MW00900034

the Mouse & the Buddha

story by Kathryn Price, illustrations by Traer Price

Little House Press

Text copyright © Kathryn Price 2006
Illustrations copyright © Traer Price 2006

Little House Press
St. Petersburg, Florida

Library of Congress Control Number: 2005935187

ISBN-13: 978-0-9773812-0-3
ISBN-10: 0-9773812-0-X

Printed in the U.S.A.
Designed by Traer Price

for Hawley, Frances and Lenore

There once was a mouse who lived with a family,
high in the mountains of Dharamsala, India.

The mouse was called Tsi Tsi.

This is Tibetan for mouse.

He was a hungry little mouse.

One night he sneaked past the sleeping

children and entered the temple

where the big gold Buddha sat.

In front of the Buddha was a feast for a king.

There were oranges, chocolates and butter

sculptures that looked like delicate flowers.

There were cookies, candies, and beautifully

baked pastries in the shape of crescent moons.

Tsi Tsi sat and ate the treats and
watched the candles and incense burn
to nothing but stubs and ash.

Oh, the Buddha loved the mouse's company. While the mouse ate, the Buddha spoke softly to the hungry creature and lovingly shared his wisdom. He said:

We all live under the same bright sun.

Be kind to others.

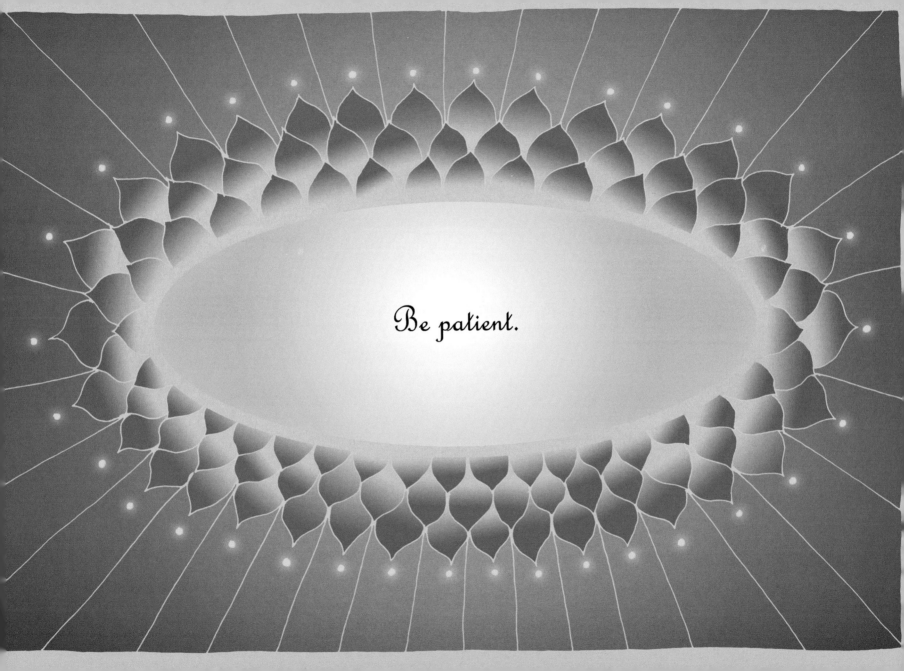

Be patient.

Have compassion for those
less fortunate than you.

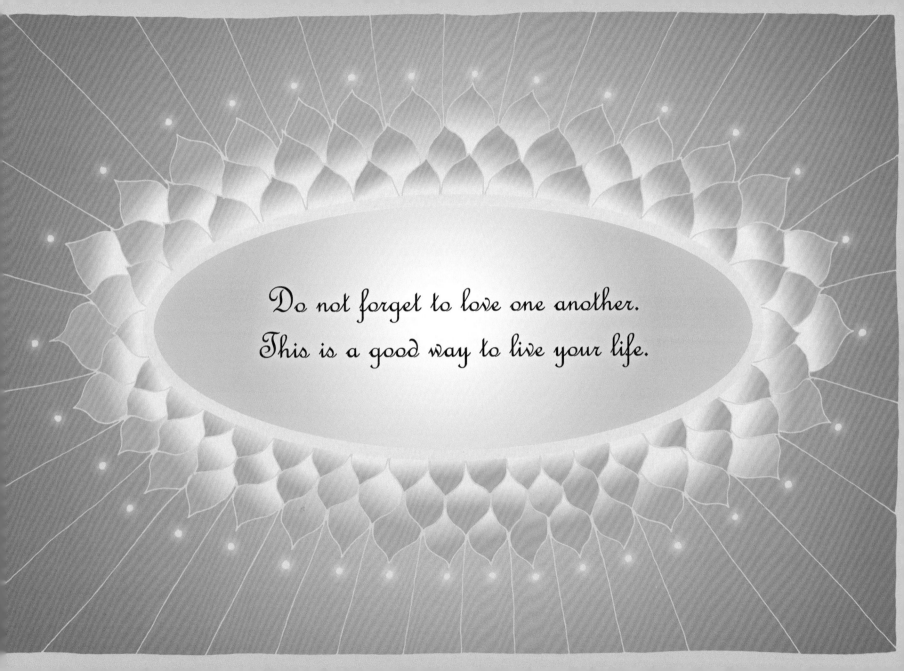

Do not forget to love one another.
This is a good way to live your life.

As the Buddha spoke, Tsi Tsi thought about
his family and friends and even the strangers
he encountered on the street. The very next day
he began to live the life the Buddha spoke of.

He planted a garden for a friend.
He helped older mice get to the market for
their bread and cheese. He visited those
who were lonely and sick.

Tsi Tsi was kind to everyone he met that day, even a cat!

The next night Tsi Tsi visited the temple again.
As he ate, he told the Buddha all he had
learned that day. When he was full and sleepy,
Tsi Tsi licked the chocolate from his paws,
wiped the pastry crumbs from his mouth
and quietly thanked the Buddha.

Before Tsi Tsi left the temple, he scratched

the Buddha on his big belly to make him laugh.

Oh, what a joyous laugh it was.

It rang through all of the great mountains

and over all the great oceans.

Later, as the little mouse drifted off to sleep, whiskers twitching, he thought about the things the big gold Buddha had shared with him.

Tsi Tsi liked one message the most.

"Do not forget to love one another,"

he whispered into the night.

And off he fell to sleep.

The End